ROYAL WOLF'S BRIDE

SHIFTER DADDIES MATES ROMANCE

AMELIA WILSON

Copyright © 2022 by SSPATEL Publishing
All rights reserved.
http://ameliawilsonauthor.com/

In no way is it legal to reproduce, duplicate, or transmit any part of this document in either electronic means or printed format. Recording of this publication is strictly prohibited, and any storage of this document is not allowed unless with written permission from the publisher. All rights reserved.

This book is a work of fiction. Names, characters, places, and incidents are either the product of the author's imagination or are used fictitiously, and any resemblance to actual persons, living or dead, events or locales is entirely coincidental.

CHAPTER ONE

Kimber

"I'm pregnant," Kimber Blackheart told her four closest friends.

All four ladies came to a halt in the kitchen at the cabin and blinked at her. Hailey placed a hand on her round belly. "How?"

"You're pregnant with my brother's twins. I'm quite sure you know how that happened," Kimber replied.

"Okay, since Mel and Jenny both have kids and I am pregnant, as you know, the question is when?" Cammie asked, with a sparkle to her green eyes.

Right. Time to come clean.

"Okay, remember when we went out for the girl's night to celebrate Cammie and Rourke's engagement?" Kimber began.

"No, I stayed home and babysat Johanna and Shaun,

so Mel and Jenny could go, and the guys could do their thing," Kimber reminded. "That was the night Cammie realized she was pregnant."

"Why do men insist on showering in cologne?" Cammie inquired in all sincerity. "God, just thinking about it makes me want to barf."

"No clue why they do it," Kimber replied. "Then again, we're shifters, so our sense of smell is better than most. Yours even more so now that you're pregnant."

"It's nasty, even for us humans," Jenny chimed in, while Mel and Hailey nodded in agreement. "So, as I recall, Mel and I took Cammie home, and you stayed at the club."

"Right, and not to sound like a tramp, that's when it happened," Kimber grinned, unable to control her smile or the flutters n her stomach just at the mere thought of him. "Male wolf testosterone, and he like me, was having a real good time. Not to mention staying in the hotel where the club was. "Believe me when I say, the man was built for sin, and wow did we have sex, like repeatedly for hours. Then the following morning, we hung out and had dinner, then more sex. It was a small miracle I could walk. The next morning is when I left him just before the sun came up."

"Sounds delicious," Mel giggled.

"It was, only I never caught his last name, or even where he's from, though he had a European accent," Kimber added. "Even now, just thinking about it makes my panties wet."

"And you're oversharing again," Hailey laughed and scrunched her nose.

"You spent over twenty-four hours with a guy and didn't get the last name?" Hailey inquired with a lift of brows.

"So, what's the problem?" Jenny sighed. "You're having a baby, aren't you excited?"

Now came the tricky part.

"Yes, I am actually, and unlike Cammie and Hailey, I haven't been sick at all."

"I always knew you were a bitch," Cammie snickered, then smiled. "It's a good thing, Hailey, and I love you," she added.

Mel exchanged a glance with Jenny and Hailey, then met Kimber's gaze. "So, do your parents know?"

Kimber groaned. "No, and neither does Jagger. You know how protective he can be."

The women all nodded. "Yes," Jenny stated. "All of them are," she reminded, referring to Jagger's three best friends Xavier Kirsch and the twins Nicco and Rourke Lombardi. All lawyers, shifters and the loves of the women Kimber now confided in.

"Wait!" Jenny exclaimed. "You're telling us and haven't told your family?"

Kimber shrugged. "I love you, and look at you as sisters, so I wanted your thoughts before I opened that can of worms,"

"Uh, that's all fine and dandy. However, I can't keep

secrets from Xavier, and Hailey is the worst liar going," Mel reminded the room.

"I'm honest to a flaw," Hailey agreed. "What am I going to do if Jagger corners me and does his cross-examination thing?"

Cammie blinked at Kimber. "I'm with Hailey on this, Rourke has worked with law enforcement, and he has the whole interrogation thing down to a science."

This wasn't helping.

"What am I going to do?" Kimber pleaded, feeling a tad out of her element. "I can't keep this a secret forever. My parents will lose their minds if they find out I'm pregnant with a baby and didn't bother to catch the surname of the father."

Jenny crossed over to her. "Breathe. We'll figure this out." She paused and debated, then continued. "So, let's get this established. You plan on keeping the baby?"

Kimber shook her head. "I like the idea of being a mom, and I know it won't be easy being single, but you and Mel both did it."

"And we didn't have you, Hailey, or Cammie," Mel encouraged.

"Or each other," Jenny added. "We support you completely."

Slowly, Kimber digested everything and knew she had the love and support of her family. "I know my parents had hopes in me marrying well. Now I'm not so sure if that will happen."

"Don't doubt, I believe in happy endings, and you'll get yours," Hailey assured. "I have a question."

"Okay, we knew it couldn't last. There is the photo-journalist we know and love," Cammie giggled.

Kimber laughed. "You forgot nosy and meddling."

Hailey rolled her eyes. "If you were having such a great time with him, why did you leave without getting the last name? Come to think of it, why did you leave him at all?"

"I got scared," Kimber confessed and crossed the floor to the walk-in pantry.

"Of what?" Cammie asked. The concern in her tone wasn't hard to miss.

She wasn't sure how honest she should be. Then again, she'd come this far. Kimber tugged open the pantry door, stepped inside, grabbed a bag of chips, and closed the door. She darted her gaze over her friends, waiting patiently. "Because he was perfect. Too perfect," she replied and opened the bag in her hand. "I guess it's because I thought love and settling down wasn't some-thing I wanted or was worthy of. The downside to being a wild child." She added, then reached in the bag of chips. "Only, I can't stop thinking about him."

Cammie exchanged a look with the others and then walked over to where Kimber had come to a stop. "I remember missing Rourke, sometimes to the point it hurt," she confessed. "If you miss him, then maybe this encounter meant more than you realized."

"It did, only now it's a little too late," Kimber whispered.

"Hailey was one of the first people to realize I was alive. She gave Rourke the courage to believe," Cammie continued.

"What if he's married or has a life, one that would make me and a baby difficult?" Kimber asked, voicing her fear aloud.

"I mistook Hailey as Rourke's fiancée. That was awkward," Cammie laughed. "But you won't know unless you at least try to find him."

"You know the guys will help. Sure Jagger might be pissed at first," Mel encouraged. "However, if anyone can find this guy, they can."

"Them and our favorite nosy photojournalist," Cammie added. "You've got this, and we've got you. It's going to be okay."

Hailey shook her head and smiled. "Once Jagger moves past wanting to kill you, or this guy, he can run interference with your parents. He put his foot down over the wedding drama."

"Because he was afraid of losing you," Mel reminded.

"No," Hailey replied. "He couldn't, not really. Jagger is my soul mate." She looked at Kimber. "When you said this guy was perfect too perfect, and you were afraid. That's why you left. You were afraid you'd met your soul mate."

"Or a sociopath serial killer," Kimber joked. She

reached into the bag, removed several chips, and crammed them all in her mouth.

"Wow, shoving food into your mouth so you can't talk," Jenny chuckled and waved a hand. "You forget we have kids. You just revealed Hailey is right."

"Big-time," Mel agreed.

Kimber decided to give the whole truth. She finished crunching then swallowed. "There is one more thing."

All eyes rested on Kimber. "What?" Mel asked as her arched brows furrowed and made her disapproving mommy face.

"I wasn't exactly honest when I told him my name. Who knows if he gave me the right one?" Kimber confessed.

"Oh dear," Jenny breathed. "What name did you give him?"

Kimber was willing to guess she looked guilty because her friends all scowled. "I told him my name was Hailey."

The sound of vehicles on the drive brought everyone to a moment of pause.

"You gave him my name?" Hailey exclaimed, mortified. "Wait till your brother finds out this one!"

"Find's out what?" Jagger's voice asked from the threshold of the cabin.

Kimber turned to her brother, who stood with Xavier, Rourke, and Nicco. "Well, funny you should your inquiring mind be wondering."

She hoped her brother didn't kill her or the hot man she wanted more than anything to see again.

The real question was, did Mick remember her or even think about her? Kimber thought of him often and was reminded of what they had shared every day.

If only she'd stayed instead of letting fear have her leave.

CHAPTER TWO

Mikhail

"I refuse to marry Suzette," Mikhail Donte stated and pulled his large frame up to his full stature as he looked into his father's steel-blue gaze.

"This is not a debate," his father, King Phillip Donte, boomed. Not only was his father the leader of the island country of Barrastu, but he was also the most revered royal wolf shifter.

Ever.

The Donte family had ruled the country since the beginning of time, and his father, like Mikhail's grandfather, was a fierce protector of family, clan, and nation. The people loved him.

"Need I remind you, your marriage to Suzette was determined when you were both children?" his father stated with a tone that bordered on a growl.

"No, I don't need a reminder; however, this brings me to my next point. I didn't have a say," Mikhail replied.

His father wasn't getting his way.

A stern expression dusted the older man's face. "I'm the king, you are my son, and you'll do as I say."

"Not this time," Mikhail told him, refusing to back down.

His father shook his head. "Suzette and her parents will be arriving any minute. This intimate formal dinner is before us announcing your engagement to our country."

"I don't give a damn what this dinner is," Mikhail's temper rose to the surface.

"You cannot do better. She comes from a noble family, one of stature, and her shifter blood is pure," his father continued. "Again, this is not up for question or debate."

"I don't love her, there is nothing there, and I can't be bound to a mate who doesn't even spark the slightest sexual chemistry," he retorted.

Immediately, his mind went to Hailey and the night they shared. Every moment they'd spent together replayed in Mikhail's mind. She was a shifter wolf, and the sex had been off the chart. Of course, it had been a full moon, which could have intensified everything.

Maybe.

"Suzette is beautiful," his father retorted.

"And then she speaks and becomes the ugliest woman on the planet." Mikhail had little care that his words were harsh. He spoke the truth.

Surprise washed over his father's face. "That was cruel."

"I'm taking leave tonight," Mikhail stated. "I'm heading back to the United States to attend to something, which means I won't be at Mother's elaborate dinner with a family I have no intention of being a part of."

"Do not embarrass the Donte name!" his father barked.

"And marrying Suzette will bring nothing but shame to this family. You see her lineage and see prestige, but she has quite the reputation among society and is known for demoralizing her staff and anyone not like her."

His father remained silent. One thing his father cherished was a character.

Mikhail paused then continued. "She is venomous and doesn't give a damn about anyone who is impoverished or hungry. She is bitter, spoiled, and is known for getting ruthless if anything or anyone stands in her way of her getting what she wants."

Again, his mind went to the woman in Vegas who had bought a sandwich and juice for a homeless man on the street. She always used her manners to the hotel staff, and when he spoke, Mikhail knew she was listening, not just hearing what he had to say, but cared.

"I don't believe what you're saying," his father shook his head.

Sometimes the older man was too predictable. "I thought you'd say that." Mikhail stepped toward his father's desk and dropped the file he'd been holding. "Evidence, proof, and everything else you might need."

"Where did you get this?"

"Your Chief of Police worked with the head of your royal guard. They had some of their most trusted men reach out to discover what they could about Suzette." He sighed and glanced at his watch. "I will see you when I get back. Give Mother my apologies."

His father looked up from the file. "Why are you doing this?"

Mikhail wanted to lie. However, it wasn't his nature. He detested liars. "Truthfully?"

The king nodded. "Of course."

Debating his words, Mikhail nodded. "I think I left my heart in Las Vegas. A thoughtful, gorgeous shifter with who I could see myself spending life and longer. I want a chance to find her because I believe she's my soulmate." He closed his eyes. "Before you speak, try and understand. I need to know if it was the Las Vegas lights, the full moon, or something real."

"Please tell me you are not going to the US by yourself," his father sighed.

"I'd planned on it," Mikhail confessed. "I survived the last time just fine. I will again."

"No. I'm sending Luke with you. He is quick with a gun as he is to shift. I want you safe." His father cleared his throat, opened his desk drawer, and withdrew a business card. "Take this," he offered. "It's a very prestigious law firm, shifter owned and extremely credible. All of the partners are from noble lineage, and I will call ahead and inform them that the royal family of Barrastu requires their aid."

Mikhail removed the heavy linen card from his father. "Why the change of heart?"

The older man smiled. "I love your mother. She is like the other half of me. When I met her, she was promised to another. Only, I couldn't imagine life without her. I fought for her. Go, try to find this girl." Again he cleared his throat. "If you don't, you will return here and marry Suzette."

Glancing at the file on his father's desk, he knew his father would be most displeased. "Don't be so sure about that."

"Fine. However, you will marry a girl of my choosing. Now go, I will explain things to your mother, but you should leave before our guests arrive."

Mikhail laughed. "That was my plan."

The Donte patriarch smiled. "Go with destiny, and good luck."

Luck. Yes, that was something Mikhail needed right after he was on the royal jet, with a stiff drink.

CHAPTER THREE

Kimber

"So let me recap," Jagger boomed in his protective brother tone. He wasn't happy. So far, though, he hadn't killed Kimber. "You went partying with Cammie, Jen, and Mel. Although they were left, you pulled one of your wild child stunts and stayed. Hooked up with a shifter and spent the next twenty-four hours with him."

Kimber nodded her head. "So far, so good."

"Except your definition of hookup is off," Nicco clarified. "This was more like an all-night and day affair."

"Nicco!" Jenny warned from near the counter where she was dicing vegetables for Cammie.

"Everyone knows I was a player, and the residents love them and leave them," Nicco responded in his defense. "You were different."

Jenny smiled at Nicco and nodded, then glanced at the giant engagement ring on her finger. "I know."

"Can we get back to the topic at hand?" Jagger asked in full lawyer cross-examination mode. "You know the one where my sister had unprotected sex with a man she never bothered to get the last name of. Did you even get his first name?"

"It's Mick," Kimber replied quietly.

"Providing he didn't give you a fake name," Hailey snorted from the stool at the breakfast bar where she and Mel munched on veggie sticks with ranch dressing.

"Ah yes," Jagger growled with displeasure. "What possessed you to give him my wife's name?"

"I never give my real one, and Hailey is a pretty name," Kimber answered.

"It is," Rourke agreed. "Cammie is thinking of it for a middle name if we have a girl."

"Really?" Hailey gasped emotionally from the table.

Cammie turned and nodded at the other woman. "Not to mention have been an amazing friend."

"Amen to that," Mel agreed as she reached for a stick of celery.

Jagger blew out a breath and pinched the bridge of his nose. "How far along are you?" he asked Kimber quietly.

"Eight weeks," she replied and knew what was coming next.

Xavier cleared his throat. "Are you sure this Mick is the father?"

Kimber nodded her head and regretted her following

words. "Yeah, I had been going through a bit of a dry spell, with helping Hailey and the moms with the weddings and enjoying the fact I had a niece and then a nephew." She hesitated. "I love clubs and hot men. True, I flirt and get promiscuous, but I'm not a slut, and don't fall into bed with men at whim." Kimber hung her head and felt a little nauseous. "He was different."

Rourke sighed and got up from where he was seated on the sofa near Xavier. He walked into the kitchen, and regret consumed Kimber. The snap of a soda opening echoed in the quiet room. Rourke walked back into the room and squatted by the chair Kimber was seated.

"Have some ginger ale and some crackers," he told her sweetly. He then passed her the can of soda and a sleeve of saltines.

Tears filled Kimber's eyes as she glanced up into Rourke's amethyst ones. "Thank you." She sipped the ginger ale and removed a cracker. "He was so much fun. I shouldn't have left like I did, but...."

Rourke glanced to Hailey, who cast him a leveled look. Rourke glanced back at Kimber. "Love can be terrifying and amazing. Sometimes you just know. Like I did with Cammie. The first time I saw her, I just knew."

"It was like that with Melanie," Xavier admitted.

"So we have a first name, and we know he is a wolf shifter. Anything you can remember?" Rourke asked, coming to a standing position.

Kimber tried to recall. "He was wearing a silk designer suit. Not a usual color, a bit more indigo than navy. When I ran my fingers through his hair, he mentioned he had it cut that morning. It was a bit shorter than he usually wore it. However, his father would be pleased."

"What hotel were you at?" Hailey asked.

"Sevigne," Kimber answered. She frowned. "We were at Paris Gems club, inside the hotel for Cammie's party. Mick was staying on the twenty-fourth floor. Gorgeous suite. Huge hot tub."

"You mentioned earlier a European accent?" Hailey pressed for more information and walked over to the coffee table, and grabbed her phone out of her purse.

"Yes," Kimber shook her head. "What is running through that brunette head of yours?"

"An idea, and possibly an ally. Height, hair, and color?" Hailey asked and met her gaze.

"Um, tall like three or four inches on me in my pink strappy shoes," Kimber replied. "I came to his shoulder in the shower. Black hair, amber eyes, like with gold flecks and the most remarkable smile, framed by deep dimples."

"That's not a hell of a lot to go on," Nicco sighed. "And more than a one-night stand."

Hailey pressed a button on her phone. "Hi Monica, it's Hailey Blackheart. I know you'll be closing soon, but by any chance, is Sergio there?"

Blackheart? Since when did Hailey have Kimber and Jagger's last name?

"Sergio, thank heavens," Hailey sighed. "No, no, my hair and nails are fine. I'm calling about a client who was in the salon about eight weeks ago, stayed on the twenty-fourth floor."

"He's not going to give out info," Xavier breathed.

"I know it was a long time ago, but he would have been your type, deep dimples, tall, dark, handsome, and a sexy European accent. Anyway, my mother was positive; it was that Italian actor, oh the one with the amber eyes, Julio Esposito. I told her it wasn't." Hailey paused. "It wasn't the actor, but you know who I'm talking about. Downright delicious, huh?"

"For a horrible liar, Hailey can sure finagle info," Melanie giggled.

"It's because they can't see the look on her face," Kimber replied.

"So, how is your nephew doing at Harvard?" Hailey asked. "Right, I'll let Jagger know. Listen, if he needs anything more, let me know, okay? Speaking of needs. I need the name of Mr. Gorgeous."

Everyone exchanged looks. Kimber knew what that meant. Hailey was calling in a favor.

"I'd love that. Yeah, text me in a bit. Kisses." Hailey ended the call. "Sergio remembers him and will text me with a name."

"Unbelievable," Jagger breathed.

"Seriously, you're surprised she is getting a name?" Rourke asked.

"No, how I didn't realize Sergio was gay," Jagger replied. "Do you think Sergio can get the name?"

Hailey nodded and smiled. "Yeah, and I'm to let you

know his nephew is getting straight A's and is grateful for what we did."

Jagger crossed the floor and placed a kiss on Hailey's lips. "We're blessed, and the kid holds promise."

"You're helping his nephew with Harvard?" Xavier chuckled. "Tell me. He's taking law."

Jagger turned and grinned at his friend. "Absolutely, got a scholarship, but it didn't cover living expenses. Hailey told me, and we made a small donation to get him through. We had lunch with him and Sergio. He mentioned he was interested in becoming a lawyer."

"And this is why the two of you are perfect for each other," Kimber informed the room. "You both have big hearts."

Hailey's phone chimed, and she glanced down. "That didn't take long." She swiped her finger across the screen. "Wow, super-hot." She glanced up and blinked at Kimber.

"You have a picture?" Mel squealed and scampered over.

Jenny and Cammie walked away from the counter and joined Mel. "Okay, I get it, Kimber, every naughty and wicked thing you may have done," Cammie whispered.

"Oh yeah," Jenny agreed. "Like damn."

"What the hell?" Jagger asked. "How can you say that?"

The girls laughed, and Hailey flipped her phone around. "Because he looks like someone you guys would be friends with."

"That's him," Kimber got tears in her eyes.

Hailey's phone rang. "Sergio, yes, that's him." Hailey paused. "Say what? I'm sorry, run that by me again."

Kimber stood and walked over to where the other women were. Cammie wrapped a reassuring arm around her shoulders.

"Thanks, this means a lot. Anyway, have a good time with the hottie David in security, and we'll have to have you both for a barbeque if things work out between you. Kisses." Hailey hung up the phone and looked at Kimber. "You're going to want to sit down."

Cammie guided Kimber over to the chair where she had been sitting.

"Mick is short for Mikhail, the credit card went through an offshore account, and the name at the check-in didn't match the card. So there is a chance it was diplomatic channels."

"Or witness protection for the wealthy," Cammie added. "Trust me, I know firsthand."

Jagger sighed. "What aren't you saying?"

"Nothing."

Kimber, like everyone else, knew Hailey was lying. "Please tell me," she pleaded with her friend.

"David, the guy in security who Sergio is seriously crushing over, discovered something while doing some snooping. The card has been used again since then." Hailey sighed. "Jagger, it took two of us to make the twins. Don't blame Mikhail. Kimber is just as responsible."

"I know," he quietly agreed. "When was the card used?"

"Promise me, you and the guys will behave," Hailey begged.

Jagger glanced at the other three men, and Kimber held her breath. Her brother again met Hailey's gaze. "We promise. When was the card used?"

"About half an hour ago, guess who's coming back to town?" Hailey sighed. "Only this time, he isn't coming alone. The booking is for two."

Kimber couldn't believe it and burst into tears. "Now I'm terrified. Maybe I was wrong. I was crazy to think I'd met my soulmate."

"No," Cammie told her and hurried over to her. "Have a little faith, no matter how hard, I know firsthand the anxiety. We don't know anything about the second person. Even if they are beautiful and wearing a gorgeous engagement ring."

Digesting Cammie's words, Kimber understood. "So now what?"

"Hailey did her part. Now we do ours," Nicco told her with a smile. "So, guys, any suggestions?"

CHAPTER FOUR

Mikhail

"You must think I'm crazy," Mikhail stated as he and Luke walked into the office building which housed Blackheart, Lombardi & Kirsch Attorneys at Law. "Traveling halfway around the world for the woman?"

"No, your highness. I believe when you know, you know. My father told me a wolf always knows." He paused, then continued. "Permission to speak freely?"

He nodded. "Of course," Mikhail replied. "And from now on, don't ask my permission. Just express your thoughts and opinions."

"Thank you." Luke met his gaze. "I think Suzette is a poor choice. Her father is a good man, but there are stories, she is ruthless behind her pretty smile. Her older brothers are believed to be vigilantes and have attacked their clan."

Mikhail nodded. "I appreciate your honesty and integrity. Your family has always been loyal to the throne."

Luke smiled. "When I took over for my dad, your father looked at me and said he wasn't comfortable being guarded by someone the same age as his son."

Grinning, Mikhail looked at the other man. "What did you say?"

"I told him I would be happy to excuse myself and allow him to have someone older and slower to protect him."

He couldn't help but laugh and could imagine the unamused expression on his royal father's face. "I like you, Luke. We're going to get along. Maybe I should put in a request to have you do my watch."

"I'd like that," the other man admitted. "So, why are we at a law firm and not a private investigator?"

Sighing, Mikhail pushed the elevator button. "Because this firm is highly recommended for our kind and one of the partners is also an investigator. I have no clue how my father came to get their name. You know my dad, though, nothing but the best."

"Yes, there is that," Luke teased as the elevator arrived and they stepped on. "Would I be able to get a social life if I took over your watch?"

Mikhail turned to Luke and laughed as the doors closed. "Help me find the girl, and I'll see what I can do."

"I don't like Suzette's family, so I'll do whatever I can." There was something off in Luke's tone. Mikhail began to wonder if there was something the other man wasn't saying. "I'm sensing a story. I'd love to hear when you're ready to tell."

Luke turned and looked at him. "There wasn't proof, but a lot of deniability. However, my gut tells me something different."

Mikhail didn't like the sound of that. "You will have my undivided attention, and I'm a firm believer in following one's instincts."

"As am I," Luke answered. "Thank you, your highness."

"Please don't call me that. I have a first name; please use it. I want to appear as normal as possible," he confessed as the elevator door opened. "Here we go," he stated and stepped off the elevator.

Luke glanced around. "The large men in suits are carrying guns," he whispered. "They aren't lawyers, but instead security."

Mikhail wasn't sure if he should be relieved or concerned. However, upon seeing the reception area, he walked a little deeper into the room. Luke hung back a bit and continued to take in the lobby. There was no debate. The style was classy and elegant with a modern twist.

The decorator had a taste.

"Mr. Donte," a male voice called as Mikhail and Luke started toward reception.

Both Mikhail and Luke turned to the voice owner, a man equal in height and build to his crossed the floor to where they stood. His suit was equally expensive.

"Welcome to Blackheart, Lombardi & Kirsch. I'm Rourke Lombardi, one of the partners." Rourke extended his hand.

Mikhail shook the hand. "This is my friend Luke Coronas."

"We've been expecting you," he replied with a sigh and motioned with a slight hand gesture to security. "This way."

They followed Rourke down the hallway to an office. Three other men in the room were as large and well dressed. One met his gaze with eyes as blue as the ocean. Behind them, the beast flickered. However, his eyes reminded him of the woman he desperately wanted to find.

"Welcome," the man with blue eyes greeted. Then, the other three men were introduced, and again, Mikhail introduced Luke.

Luke met his gaze and nodded. He approved of their present company. Looking at the men who had nothing but cordial, they were the type of people Mikhail would choose to spend time with.

"Can we get either of you something to drink?" Nicco, undoubtedly Rourke's twin, offered.

"I'm good, thank you," Mikhail replied. "Let's not waste time," he stated. "How did you know who I was?"

"We had it on the authority you'd be arriving before your father contacted my dad," Xavier explained.

Mikhail exchanged a glance with Luke, then met the gaze of Xavier. "How so?"

"Research," the man named Jagger replied. "I'm most curious how your father obtained the name of this firm."

"That, I do not know the answer. However, much like you, I'm curious about the answer." Mikhail answered. "What kind of research?"

"Fair enough." A warm smile crossed Jagger's mouth. "As to how I knew you would be arriving, my future wife found out from the hotel."

"So much for discretion," Mikhail huffed. "Should I sue?"

Nicco chuckled. "Hailey can be persuasive when she wants. I ensure your best interest was at heart."

His throat dried, and his heart stopped. "You said, Hailey?" Again, he and Luke exchanged a look. His companion didn't look impressed. He returned his gaze to Jagger. "You said, future wife?"

An invisible weight settled on his chest.

"I did, give me one minute," Jagger replied and withdrew his phone and hit the button. "Can you come to Rourke's office, please?" There was a pause. "No, everything is fine," he assured gently. Jagger laughed. "Well, that can wait." He ended the call and glanced at his three partners. "She is on her way."

The office door opened, and Luke turned, then immediately stood. A strange expression worked across his face.

"You wished to see me," a soft female voice inquired. However, it didn't belong to the woman of Mikhail's memories.

He also rose as Jagger stood. Risking feeling like a

fool, he turned to see a stunning brunette with doe-like eyes, long lashes, and very pregnant. She walked over to Jagger and smiled sweetly, then turned to Mikhail. "Hello, my guess is I'm not who you were expecting."

"Definitely not, mio bella," he assured and stepped toward the lovely. "It is a pleasure to make your acquaintance, I'm Mikhail, and the man with me is Luke."

"The pleasure is mine," she stated in a kind and sincere manner. He cast her a glance over. Everything about her revealed money and class.

"You are here in search of a woman," Rourke began. "However, we already know who it is you are looking for, and her name isn't Hailey. No more than yours is Mick, which is what you told her and much more blue-collar sounding than your actual name, which is far more exotic, upper-class sounding, wouldn't you agree, your highness?"

Mikhail threw his head back and laughed. He then met Hailey's gaze. "Tell me, mio bella, did a friend borrow your name?"

"I do like a smart man," she answered with a flutter of lashes. "Yes, and if I hadn't known her for over half my life, I probably would have caned her."

Luke chuckled and turned to Jagger. "She's got fire."

"That's politely putting it," the man next to Hailey replied. The other partners of the firm laughed.

"Mikhail, Luke, please know that my friend is not a liar by nature. She is a good friend," Hailey began. "The closest thing I had to a sister for many years. Las Vegas is a transient city with approximately forty million visitors a year. In perspective, that is roughly the population of California or the country of Canada. I can see how she wasn't honest about her name, but it was more for her protection rather than malicious intent."

"She's as smart as she is beautiful," Mikhail told Jagger. "I understand her connection with your sister."

He then rested his gaze on Hailey. "Are you an attorney as well?"

The pretty brunette giggled and shook her head she wasn't.

"Hailey is a former photojournalist," Nicco clarified. "And a stickler for the truth, she and Rourke work remarkably well together to get the information we need."

"You're a reporter?" Luke questioned in seriousness.

"Was," Hailey corrected. "However celebrity columns and gossip were not my forte, so you both can relax. The unjust and exposing issues like war, poverty, human trafficking, and bringing things people don't know or deny their existence to the forefront was my specialty."

Mikhail exchanged an impressed expression with Luke. He could only imagine the horrors Jagger's pretty fiancée had seen. Both he and Luke turned back to the others. "Does your sister know I will be here?"

"Actually, she doesn't," Xavier stated. "She knows that we are looking for you and that you will be staying at the same hotel as you were eight weeks ago."

Luke darted a glance to Hailey. "Your research is thorough."

"I need to know one thing," Jagger asked in seriousness. "Why are you looking for my sister? You could have any woman you want."

Mikhail debated his words. "I could indeed have any woman. However, the one I want is here. Had she too been visiting, I would have scoured the earth looking for her. I would have asked for your help. Despite the fact we were not entirely honest about our names, something deep inside tells me she is the one to spend my life with."

"We understand," Rourke assured with a smile. "I knew the moment I laid eyes on my future wife, Cammie. She was the one."

Nicco nodded. "We understand. As shifters, I believe we know, that the beast within recognizes his mate. Hailey, would you be so kind?"

"Of course, if you'll all excuse me," she stated and gracefully left the office, closing the door behind. My fiancée Cammie and I started dating in high school. Her family went into witness protection, but for almost fifteen years, I believed she was dead."

Mikhail exchanged a look with Luke, and both rested their attention on the man with Amethyst eyes.

"When I found out she was alive, so many emotions ran through me." Rourke inhaled a deep breath. "She was as scared and unsure as I was, but like me, she always believed I was the one. Like I told the young lady about to walk through the door, love is scary, but it's also amazing."

The door of the office opened.

Mikhail turned. Standing next to Hailey was the girl

he'd traveled halfway across the world to find. "It's you," he breathed. She was more beautiful than he remembered.

Her blue eyes lit up, and she nodded. "It's me."

Mikhail stepped closer to her. "Good, then would you be so kind as to give me the right name this time?"

The lovely woman standing with her pretty friend inched a little forward in his direction. "Hi Mikhail, I'm Kimber Blackheart."

CHAPTER FIVE

Kimber

Kimber held her breath. Her heart thudded fast and hard in her chest as she waited for the man she couldn't get off the brain to respond.

"Kimber," he rolled her name off his tongue, and with his accent was the sexiest sound she had ever heard. "It suits you," he told her and closed the distance between them, then reached for her hand. "Why did you leave?"

She glanced at Hailey, who now stood by Jagger, then met Mikhail's amber gaze again. "I got scared. You were too good to be true."

"I see, I don't understand, but I do get the whole concept of being unsure." He paused and sighed. "I returned here to find you, and what concerns me is this was far easier than I anticipated."

Before Kimber could respond, the echoing of a phone

ringing filled the room. The man with Mikhail and whose name she hadn't been told reached into his pocket and withdrew a cellphone from his inside suit pocket. "Hello, your highness," he greeted.

Highness?

She returned her gaze to Mikhail. "Who is that and who is the highness to who he is referring?" Kimber asked just above a whisper.

"That is Luke, he is technically my security detail, and the highness would be my father. He is the king of Barrastu," Mikhail explained.

He was kidding. "You're a prince?" The question fell off Kimber's tongue.

Guilt washed over Mikhail's handsome face. "I am."

Nerves fluttered in the pit of Kimber's stomach, and she shook her head. No, this wasn't good. Sure, most girls in her position would be thrilled to have the attention of a prince. However, Kimber wasn't that girl. She had a life here, with friends and her family. Though Kimber had traveled the world, she always knew she could return home at any time. Undoubtedly, being the mate of a prince would cause complications.

"What do you mean there was a security breech?" Luke exclaimed and exchanged a look with the other men in the room.

Jagger's back stiffened, and he darted a glance in Kimber's direction.

"We're at Blackheart, Lombardi & Kirsch Attorneys at

Law, now," Luke explained. "Do they know where we were going?"

Kimber glanced at Mikhail. "What don't I know?"

Mikhail's handsome face was etched in concern. "I have some things I need to tell you," he breathed.

She thought of her pregnancy and debated her following words. "That makes two of us," she added and wondered if being honest about the father of her baby had been wise. Of course, she still had to tell Mikhail.

What if he didn't believe the baby was his?

"What's wrong?" Mikhail asked gently.

"Just nerves," she replied honestly, trying to push all self-doubt out of her mind.

"I agree," Luke concurred with whatever the conversation was at the other end of the phone. "I will discuss with the others the best course of action, and I assure you, both the prince and his intended shall be safe."

Safe? Oh, what the hell, now?

Mikhail stepped away from her as Luke ended the call. "What?"

"There was a security breech. Baron Saracens found out you didn't attend dinner because you were returning to Las Vegas. He finds it unbecoming for the man to marry his daughter. Suzette threw a tantrum and said nothing or anyone is going to stop her from marrying you."

"Marrying?" Kimber stumbled back. Jagger stiffened, and the look on his face became lethal. The beast behind his eyes flickered.

"No, not this lifetime or any other," Mikhail assured. He glanced at Jagger. "I can explain."

"Please," her brother replied tersely, then glanced at his three closest friends. Jagger's expression was down murderous.

Kimber's heart ached, and she wanted to cry. "Your friend Luke here just said—"

"I swear to you," Mikhail began. "It's not what you think. "My parents promised me to another woman when I was a child. It was to strengthen our clan. My father knows I am here. He knows I don't love Suzette. I swear on my mother's life, I have never had any relations with her and have never shared a bed."

Kimber remembered the time they had spent together on Mikhail's last visit. He was incredibly close to his mother as well as his aunts.

"The Baron Saracens offsprings are not of character. His daughter is a wretched bitch," Luke glanced at Hailey and Kimber. "My apologies, ladies, for the coarse language."

"No apology needed," Hailey assured with a nervous smile.

Kimber wasn't sure what to think and suddenly felt light-headed. "I need to sit,' she whispered.

Concern and worry washed over Mikhail's face, and he gently captured her arm and had her sit in one of the plush chairs. "You're pale," he told her quietly.

"How bad are the shifters coming to Las Vegas?" Xavier asked. There was no denying he was displeased.

Luke sighed and shook his head. "The worst of wolf shifters. They have killed others not only outside their pack but members of their clan. They are deadly to anyone who stands in the way of what they want."

"And their sister?" Nicco asked with trepidation.

"Is lovely at first sight then when she speaks, its venom, and she becomes uglier with every word spoken," Mikhail told them coldly. "She only wants to marry well, and nothing better than a prince. She doesn't love me, and now I fear for Kimber's safety." Mikhail knelt by her and smiled, though the gesture didn't quite reach his gorgeous eyes. "I will fight for you," he assured, then studied her.

"What is it?" she asked with hesitation.

"You look good, but there is something different about you," he explained.

Hailey cleared her throat.

Mikhail glanced at Kimber's best friend then returned his attention to Kimber. "Tell me, il mio cuore, what is it you were going to tell me?"

She wasn't sure what to think of the situation. However, the hottie wolf prince had conveyed sincerity. Mingling with his high-end cologne was a concern. "I'm pregnant," she revealed in a tone not much more than a whisper.

Surprise washed over Mikhail's face.

Kimber hadn't meant to blurt it out. "Before you ask, it's yours. I'll take whatever test you want to prove it," she added, bordering on catatonic.

"There won't be any need for that," he told her with a

soothing tone, then tucked a strand of hair behind her. "I believe you, and I want you, Kimber. However, now I'm twice as concerned for your safety and our child's." Mikhail curled his fingers around her hand. "We'll figure this out, I promise."

"You know I'll protect her," Luke stated in all seriousness. "Just as I would you."

Xavier sighed. "What can we do to help?"

Jagger smiled and nodded. "We have experience with women in jeopardy." He debated and glanced at Hailey before meeting Mikhail's gaze. "I never thought Kimber would be one of them. She fought for Cammie, Rourke's future wife as well as Hailey."

"How many rooms are on your floor of the hotel?"

Mikhail turned to Rourke. "Two. One at each end. Why?"

"I'll call the hotel and make sure the second room is vacated," Jagger stated. "We'll use that as a base. Since I'm sure, you're going to want some time alone with my sister. We'll be close, but not invasive unless we need to be."

"I like this idea," Luke told them. "If the room is booked. Mikhail will pay for any upgrades or show tickets or whatever is required."

Kimber processed the conversation around her then turned to Hailey. "How did you do it?" she asked her friend quietly. "You didn't have an animal beneath? I do, and I'm scared."

"You're human?" Mikhail asked Kimber's friend in surprise.

Hailey's back stiffened, then nodded; however, sadness touched her features. "Yes," she replied quietly.

"You're lovely, smart, and demonstrate empathy," Mikhail told her. "In Barrastu, my country, mixed marriages are common. I have two remarkable aunts who are human, and both are a force to be reckoned with."

"My mother is human," Luke informed the room.

"Hailey still gets a little unsure of herself," Kimber explained. "Xavier and Nicco's mates are human, so it helps, but she is still a bit sensitive in some circles."

"Please, not around Luke or I," Mikhail encouraged. He glanced at Kimber. "If I had my way, I would ship you off to someplace remote."

"If I need, I can go to my aunt's or Haley's parents in California," Kimber stated as nerves fluttered in her stomach and made her nauseous. "However, I'm pregnant, not dead, and I didn't know if I would see you again. Now that you're here, I'm not leaving you."

Mikhail's long dark lashes fluttered, and he blinked at her. A wry smile worked across his lips. The same mouth Kimber longed to kiss. He then turned to Jagger. "Is she always this stubborn?"

Her brother laughed. "No, she can be much worse."

"Well then, I do believe I truly have met my match," Mikhail stated. "So, how do you want to proceed?"

CHAPTER SIX

Kimber

Kimber inhaled a deep breath as she stepped into the hotel room. Only eight weeks ago, she had been in this room with Mikhail and had experienced the best time of her life. Fear had her leave, but she had changed in the time she'd spent with Mikhail. For a fleeting moment, life was perfect, and the thought terrified her.

"Are you okay?" Mikhail asked as he draped his suit jacket over a sofa, then stepped toward her.

She nodded and studied him a moment. "I will be." She debated her following words. "I missed you and what we shared," she exclaimed.

A wide grin curled across the mouth of the large, gorgeous man in front of her. "I missed you too," he replied and closed the distance between them. His strong arms wrapped around her waist, and he tugged her close, so her breasts came against his solid chest.

She rested her head against his shoulder and savored the safety of his muscular body, holding her against him. Kimber sighed. "Are you sure you're okay about the baby?" she asked with hesitation.

Mikhail eased her back just a bit and met her gaze. "More than okay, I'm happy, and my mother is going to be thrilled." He flashed her a wicked grin, which emphasized his deep dimples on either side of his perfect smile. "Besides, if you weren't pregnant when I finally found you, I definitely would have worked on changing that," he replied with a wink.

His head lowered, and his warm, firm mouth grazed her lips. Again, he pulled her closer as he deepened the kiss and his tongue started to explore her mouth. Desire pooled between Kimber's legs, and her body ignited in passion. A slight sense of relief eased the tension in her shoulders, and her muscles relaxed. She enjoyed the taste of him and wrapped her arms around his neck.

Finally, he lifted his mouth from hers. "Can I get you anything? A glass of juice?"

"Please," she replied. "Jagger and the guys said they would get take out, which I am hoping is something spicy, but I'd love some pineapple juice.

"Anything. I mean anything you want, Kimber, I don't want you to want for anything," Mikhail told her with a gentle tone as he walked over to the wet bar of the luxury suite. "Are you getting the rest and care you need? What about medical? I can have the best doctor's in the world make sure you and the baby have looked after."

For a second, she was overwhelmed. Then again, she had fallen for a prince. What did she expect?

"The baby is fine. I think my pregnancy is so far, so good," she admitted to him. "I do feel a bit overwhelmed, and I know you'll have royal obligations in Barrastu, but I love my family and friends here, and I only dared to find you because of them."

Mikhail's expression softened, and he sighed. "I want you happy, healthy, and safe."

Kimber nodded and tried wrapping her head around the situation. Overnight she had gone from staining her pillow with tears, believing to the root of her soul she'd missed out on the man to be her soulmate. Now, she was with him again and had thought about her as much as she had thought about him.

"So, you came back to Vegas to have my family's law firm help you find the woman—which turned out to be me." Kimber paused and thought. "Don't you find it a touch convenient that your father gave you a Blackheart, Lombardi & Kirsch Attorneys at Law business card?"

Mikhail paused and met her gaze from across the room. "Knowing that you are related, yes, I find it more than a little suspicious. Your brother was as curious as me as to how my father attained the card." He debated then continued. "Yet my father called Xavier's father. Even more interesting."

"Maybe not," Kimber supplied. "Xavier is a dragon shifter. From royal lineage."

The sexy prince absorbed this information. "Go on, il mio cuore, please." A slow smile curled across his lips. "I understand your friendship with Hailey. She is smart, as are you. As my future wife, I want to hear what you think and care about your opinion, as I told your brother. I truly get your friendship with your brother's future wife."

"Hailey is the closest thing I had to a sister. We went to the same prestigious boarding school. I was her first exposure and experience with shifters, and I knew somehow she was destined to be part of my life." She thought about her friend and her brother. "Both Hailey and my brother have generous hearts and will fiercely fight for those they love. I also know my brother respects Hailey and her thoughts."

Mikhail nodded in agreement. "My father values my mother's thoughts, as do my uncles with my aunts. So you as well find it suspicious I was directed to your family's firm."

Kimber stepped closer to the bar and accepted the s glass of pineapple juice Mikhail held out. "Do you think your dad had you followed the last time you came to Las Vegas?" She thought some more of what she knew.

"I admit, finding you was easier than I anticipated," Mikhail told her honestly. "Maybe my father did have me followed. I thought I had dodged the security detail rather effectively. However, now I wonder." He pondered a moment. "This is all too convenient."

Kimber wasn't sure how she felt about the last statement but tried not to read too much into it, either way.

Mikhail exhaled a breath. "I just hope that we find Suzette's brothers before they find us, and I truly hope Suzette isn't with them." There was grave concern in Mikhail's tone.

"You're worried."

"Very," he responded without hesitation.

"She doesn't seem stable," Kimber disclosed before sipping her juice.

"No, I don't think she is," Mikhail admitted. "She is evil, and her father makes excuses for her." He heaved a sigh, and a worrisome expression crossed his handsome face. "The last time I was here. No. Let me back up. I asked my father's Chief of Police and my father's royal guard to look into Suzette's past discreetly. I basically dodged all security—or so I thought, and came here."

Kimber nodded, knowing to her root, that Mikhail was explaining for a reason. The animal within her stirred, but instead of interrupting, she let him continue. She took a seat on one of the stools by the bar as Mikhail walked around.

"Something about spending my life with someone, which left me with an unsettling feeling, wasn't right. She wasn't all she appeared." He took a seat next to Kimber and reached out. Mikhail gently curled his fingers around the hand, not holding her glass. "I wanted answers and to get away from Suzette, so left the task in my trusted hands and came here. Out of all the places in the world, something said Las Vegas."

"I'm sorry I got scared and left without saying goodbye," she confessed in a full-hearted apology. "I didn't know life could be like it was. The way we talked with ease and the chemistry between us was mind-blowing. You wined, dined, and held a conversation, and when I spoke, you listened and just didn't hear me."

"Kimber, now that I have you, I don't want to let you go, but the Saracens clan is ruthless," Mikhail stated. "Is there any way I can convince you to go to your aunt's or Hailey's family in California?"

Tears filled her eyes, and she blamed the changes her body was going through with her pregnancy for a fleeting moment. "I don't want to leave you."

Mikhail gently squeezed her fingers in reassurance. "I understand. I don't want to be away from you either. However, I'm worried about you and our child."

Kimber studied the emotional expression on Mikhail's face. "We have time before my brother and Luke deal with dinner." She glanced down at her hand still in her prince charming, then again, met his gaze. "Tell me something, do you believe in love at first sight?"

CHAPTER SEVEN

Mikhail

Kimber's question surprised him, but he loved the fact that they still talked like old friends despite the weeks and the developments. "I never believed in love at first sight," Mikhail whispered. "Then there you were."

His future princess's blue eyes illuminated, and a thoughtful expression crossed her beautiful features. "When you were here weeks back, you mentioned, you needed to blow off steam and get away." Hesitation dusted across her pretty face. "You came here to get away from your marriage. I can't say I blame you."

"Yes," he admitted. "I promise you, Kimber, all I want is you."

A sultry smile danced across her full lips. "Not only do I want you too, but I also want to be yours," she confessed. The last words left her mouth in a breathy whisper. "Hailey never dated. She was resistant to any thoughts of a relationship. Jagger had watched Xavier lose Melanie and Rourke losing Cammie. Never did he want to endure the pain both those men endured. Of course, he wasn't a player, unlike Nicco, who could never see him with one woman—until Jenny and her son came along, and then they were all he wanted."

Mikhail loved hearing about the people who Kimber loved and cherished. "Go on, please."

Kimber smiled sweetly. "Then Hailey had a lion shifter and an evil dragon shifter after her. However, I took her to get help from my brother and the guys. I swear, it took just one look." She giggled and shook her head. "I mean, I'd been trying to get them together for months, a blind date if you will. Zero interest or energy on either one's part. All it took was one look in his office, and it was like time stood still."

"That's how I felt when I saw you," he confessed. "It was like the room around me faded away. All I saw was you, and I had to know who you were and say something because never in my life had the world stopped around me. Maybe that's when I knew you were the one. My destiny."

Desire fluttered back at him in her blue eyes, between her long lashes. Kimber placed her glass on the granite surface of the bar and slid out of the stool. She wrapped her arms around his neck and grazed her lips against his mouth.

He could smell her arousal, pure Luna female—the

perfect wolf mate, and his groin stirred. "I want you," he told her in a husky whisper.

A naughty and remarkably sexy expression worked across her pretty face. "We have time to explore that before dinner." Kimber giggled. "Why don't you have me for your appetizer?"

Memories of their time together weeks ago flashed through his mind. Images of her naked on the bed writhing beneath him stiffened his groin. Mikhail stood, and his body grazed against Kimber's soft curves. Her lashes fluttered closed while Mikhail leaned in and claimed her lips in a heated kiss. His cock was already rock-hard as he pressed it against the flesh of her belly. She moaned against his tongue.

His body craved and longed for more of her. Even though he'd had her just under eight weeks ago, it felt like a lifetime ago. Mikhail had woke to her gone, and from that moment on, his heart had ached. Like his soul was missing a chunk, and he would never get it back.

Now that Mikhail had Kimber, he was never letting her go. He originally was going to wait until after dinner, but knowing she had missed him as he missed her, and she was having his baby made his desire even more intense.

The way her body flamed and responded to his slightest caresses, she wanted him as bad as he needed her.

He longed to experience more of her, like he had,

only this time he'd be claiming her as his mate. Maybe not biding legally, but she was his.

Mikhail ran his hands down her back and cupped her firm ass. Kimber's legs wrapped around his waist, and he carried the short distance into the bedroom. She removed her legs, and slid to the floor, then glided her hands to his strong shoulders. Kimber's hands caressed across his upper chest to the top buttons of his silk dress shirt, then trailed her fingers down the fabric, undoing the buttons as she went down. The fabric parted, and her gentle touch shifted from his dress shirt to the skin of his chest.

Mikhail shrugged out the garment and let it fall to the floor. Kimber her gaze raked over his body. The way she stared at him was with pure primal lust. The animal behind her eyes flickered in the blue depths.

He hoped at that moment that their baby had her eye color.

Kimber's carnal stare worked over his flesh like flames across his skin. Her gaze met his again as he tugged her blouse up and over her head, then dropped it to the floor. Mikhail stroked his hands over the soft lace of her bra and squeezed the smooth, round breasts beneath the fabric. His fingers dipped to the center clasp and sprung her full breasts free, her nipples already aroused and hard. He then shoved the lingerie off her shoulders, so it too landed with the other discarded clothing.

Her fingers curled around his belt and undid the buckle, then the button and zipper of his dress pants. He stepped out of her reach and then slipped off his dress pants and boxer briefs. His dick sprung free, aching and straining erect.

Mikhail lightly kissed her lips as he slowly undid her jeans and removed them and her panty, which matched her bra, exposing her bald pussy. He reached out and grabbed her hips, then gently eased her back onto the bed.

Before she could move, Mikhail glided his body over hers and grabbed one of her perky breasts. He cupped it in his hand, flicked his tongue across it then sucked the taught peak. Kimber's body writhed beneath him in pleasure. She arched her back and pressed more of her flesh into his mouth. Her movement had her pussy lips teased the head of his cock.

Despite wanting to bury himself deep inside of her, he dragged the head of his erection back and forth over her slick wet folds. Kimber moaned, and Mikhail lowered his face down and snaked his tongue over the spot his dick had trailed.

Pre-cum seeped from his throbbing dick. Her head pressed against the pillow and her back arched again while her legs spread, giving him easier access.

Kimber tasted good, and after Mikhail pressed his mouth to her aroused body, he thrust his tongue inside her pussy. His cock begged to be inside her, but he loved how her soft flesh shifted and stirred to his tongue and mouth, devouring her pussy. Another moan escaped her, and she rocked her hips. Mikhail's movements picked up speed, and her breaths became shallow and rapid. Kimber's knees bent, and a soft wail left her as her body trembled.

Mikhail clamped his mouth hard against her pussy, which twitched around his tongue. Liquid coated his tongue as her climax washed over her body in a fierce tremble. He licked and gently laved before again stretching his body over the length of hers and covering her mouth for another kiss. Kimber's soft hands trailed over his shoulders and then shifted him back and ended the kiss.

She shifted her body weight, eased his shoulders back onto the bed, and then hoovered her body over his. Her tongue caressed down his throat, then slid the velvety smoothness over his collar bone and then down the center of his chest. Glancing up, she cast a sultry smile.

"You have the sexiest grin," Kimber whispered.

"That's funny. I was thinking the same about you," he teased.

Longing, smoldered in her dark eyes, and Mikhail took in every detail of her pretty face. "You're incredible and going to be mine."

"In so many ways, I'm already yours," she licked her lips and then placed a hot wet kiss again against the skin of his chest. Even though Mikhail liked to be in control, Kimber's body, full mouth, and tongue felt incredible against his skin, and his body burned in arousal.

Mikhail groaned as her hand circled his throbbing dick and gently stroked up and down the length.

Kimber raked her tongue seductively over the head and then continued its sensual, wet caress down to her fingers resting at the base.

He moaned in pleasure. His body had craved her in all the time he'd missed her. She slithered her mouth over the tip, then thrust him entirely into her mouth. Mikhail darted a glance down, and her blue gaze sparkled up at him with a hunger that strengthened the pleasure working over his body.

Her tongue seductively and systematically worked over his hard dick as her pouty, full lips rocked his dick in a steady rhythm with her hand gliding up and down. Mikhail bucked his hips upward, pushing toward her mouth and enticing a moan to leave her, and buried his cock all the way in.

The vibration traveled down his length to his balls.

Pressure built in Mikhail's sac as he was forced to hold back, erupting in the hot cavern of her mouth, answering the call of her licking and sucking lips adoring his cock. He reached down and seized her under the arms, then gently lifted her off him. Mikhail pulled her toward him.

Kimber's hard nipples and full, perky breasts rested against his body. Kimber shifted her hips and legs so that the tip of his cock seeped with pre-cum pressed against her. Her wet folds parted, and he stretched her wet core as she lowered down over him.

She worked her pussy up and down his aching erection, then leaned forward, so her breasts came against his chest. Mikhail grasped her hips and gently rocked her, thrusting his hips up into her rhythmic movements. His grip tightened on her, plunging deeper into her wetness.

She whimpered in pleasure and placed her palms flat against his chest before grinding his dick a little faster. Mikhail started to thrust harder, deeper, and more speed into her. He wanted her to orgasm again and brought on his release. He struggled not to ejaculate as Kimber's walls squeezed tight around him.

Kimber's hair tossed back off her face as her head tilted back, and a loud wail left her full lips as her curvy frame trembled. She braced herself against him as her release coated his cock, still working in and out of her. She was too tight and felt too good.

Mikhail couldn't hold back anymore and slammed into her as his orgasm pumped hard and fast into her pussy. Again, Kimber trembled in response to his orgasm before she lowered her head to his chest. Kimber's heart thudded hard and as fast as his and her breaths were equally as ragged.

The skin of Kimber's soft cheek rested against his chest. He lifted a hand and gently caressed her hair. Mikhail believed things would work out between them even though Suzette's brothers were coming for them both.

Right now, Mikhail just wanted to hold the woman he knew was destined to be his from the moment he first laid eyes on her in the busy club. The woman who was carrying his child and he would protect at all costs. He lowered his hand and wrapped an arm around her.

There was no denying the truth. Love at first sight existed, and he was definitely in love with Kimber.

Mikhail always would be. Somehow they had to survive this. Hopefully, her brother and the other attorneys had some ideas.

Before they did anything, they would need a shower. However, Mikhail wasn't in a hurry to get up. Right now, he just wanted to hold Kimber.

CHAPTER EIGHT

Kimber

Mikhail held Kimber's hand as they walked down the hotel hallway to the other room they shared the hotel floor with. After the incredible sex and a quick shower, Kimber was starving. She should have blown-dried her hair; however, none of the men they were about to meet with were stupid. Undoubtedly they already suspected she would have sex with Mikhail.

The smell of Chinese food wafted into the hallway, and her mouth watered. "I hope they ordered orange chicken," she whispered as Mikhail knocked on the door.

He flashed her a sexy grin, and her heart skipped a beat.

Xavier pulled open the door, and he waved them in. He met Kimber's gaze. "Are you doing okay?"

She smiled and nodded. "We're doing well, but I'm

starving," she told the dragon shifter, who she cherished like a brother.

"Of course you are," Rourke chuckled over by the bar where the food was set up. "Come on and get something to eat."

Kimber glanced over to the sitting area, where the others talked quietly. Luke was on the phone, and Jagger and Nicco discussed something calmly. Worry settled in, and she glanced at the food.

"Hey," Mikhail soothed as if reading her mind. He darted a look to Jagger, Luke, and Nicco. Then his amber gaze again rested on Kimber. "Il mio cuore, they are doing their job," he told her quietly. "Now, why don't you get yourself and our baby something to eat?"

More than anything, Kimber wanted to know what was going on. However, the food smelled good.

Mikhail placed a light kiss on the back of her hand. "Please."

She knew in her heart he was worried. Kimber nodded, releasing Mikhail's hand. She turned to Xavier. "I hope there is orange chicken."

"There is, and that spicy seafood soup, Jagger said, was your favorite," Xavier informed.

Kimber walked over to the bar, immediately swiped a spring roll, and bit into the delectable Asian appetizer. Rourke chuckled, and she knew he was studying her. "You look good. How are you feeling?" he asked as he passed her a paper plate, but she didn't take it.

She darted a glance to where Mikhail and Xavier had

joined the others. They talked quiet enough across the room that she couldn't hear what was discussed. Finally, she turned back to Rourke. "I'm starving, a little unnerved. I miss the girls, and despite the fact he was promised to another woman, I know he's the one."

"Kimber, we had a chance to talk to him before you walked into the office and just saw how he treats you. Then just now. He cares about you," Rourke told her with a smile.

"He's the one," she whispered, then took another bite of the spring roll.

Rourke nodded. "I believe you." A sweet smile worked across his face. "You've been there for us. Not to mention, the only girl."

"Sometimes, it felt like I had four older brothers instead of just one. That's why Hailey is so important to me," Kimber explained. "However, you, Nicco, and Xavier, as annoying as you were when we were younger, have landed you amazing mates. I know have four remarkable women I look at as sisters."

A slow, deliberate breath left Rourke's mouth. "You know I did my due diligence on Mikhail. He's not only a standup guy. He's a genuinely nice guy. He cares about his people. Especially those in impoverished areas of the country."

Kimber digested this information. She hadn't learned much about Mikhail's role in his country. "He sounds like he's compassionate and someone you all would be friends with."

"Yeah," he chuckled. "Let me do you up a plate." He studied her a moment longer. "I maybe miss the girls, more than I let on. This is all new and a whole lot scary as it is exciting." She glanced back over at the guys whispering.

Never had she been one to sit on the sidelines. She had been there for both Hailey and Cammie. Kimber would have fought Melanie's father next to Rourke, Nicco, and Xavier for Johanna, Mel, and Xavier's daughter. She would have gone with Nicco and Jagger the day they saved Jenny from a stalker.

Now Kimber was the possible target, and she wouldn't be silenced.

"Could you bring the plate over to the sofa? I want to sit and something more comfortable," she told Rourke.

He narrowed his gaze. "No, your real motive is to find out what's going on."

She snickered, then shrugged before flashing him a grin. "Well, there is that too," she giggled and swiped another spring roll. Though there was much about Mikhail, like his royal duties, she didn't know. However, she knew he loved spring rolls. Kimber walked over to where Mikhail sat with the other four men.

True, she felt outnumbered and debated calling Hailey. She approached the men, and the conversation came to a halt. "I don't mean to interrupt," she told them in her usual sassy tone and plunked herself on the sofa next to Mikhail. She held up the spring roll in front of

Mikhail's mouth. He flashed her a grin, framed by his deep dimples, then took a bite.

Slowly he chewed, then swallowed. "That is one of the best spring rolls I've ever had."

Nicco chuckled. "They are. The restaurant we ordered from was the first Chinese restaurant in Las Vegas and still has some of the most amazing dishes in town."

"Nicco fails to mention that the restaurant was here before Las Vegas was and rumors are the restaurant that stands in town today, its actual origins date back to 1905," Kimber explained. "When the first Chinese miners made their way to Nevada. Whether it's true or not, their spring rolls are amazing, and the spicy seafood soup is incredible."

Mikhail smiled. "I love how you know random pieces of history."

"It's what had Hailey, and I first become friends back in boarding school," she told him, remembering back to their teen years. "We both loved history and useless knowledge and hated our school uniforms," she told him. "I wish she was here."

Mikhail chuckled. "No knowledge is useless. I'm most curious about the school uniform now. You'll have to show me pictures sometime."

"Definitely not," she laughed and shoved the rest of the spring roll in her hand into his mouth.

"Have no fear," Jagger began. "My mother will be

happy to crack open the photo albums, and if she doesn't, I will."

After swallowing the mouthful of food, Mikhail looked at Jagger and then turned to Kimber. "I like your brother."

Kimber giggled. She suspected that the man of her dreams would get along with her family. "I'd like to say I'm surprised."

Rourke brought over a plate of food and a set of chopsticks. She blinked and looked up at him. "No soup?"

"Why don't you start with this and work up to the soup," he told her with a smile. "I would hate for you to have pregnancy regret."

She rolled her eyes. "I haven't had morning sickness. I'll be fine."

"You haven't been sick at all?" Mikhail asked in quiet sincerity.

Kimber met his amber gaze and shook her head. "No, much to Cammie and Hailey's dismay."

Mikhail glanced at the other men then looked back at Kimber. "Why don't you have a couple of bites, and then I'll grab you one of the soup."

Something in his tone set her nerves on edge. "What's going on?" She asked, placing the plate on the coffee table then removing the wooden chopsticks from the paper wrapper.

"We have confirmation the Saracen men are here in Las Vegas," Mikhail told her calmly. "The Las Vegas Metropolitan Police department is working with the royal guard ad my father's chief of Police. For clarification, the chief of Police in Barrastu is an official position, and all precincts and jurisdictions in the country report to him, and he reports directly to my father and the captain of the royal guard."

Kimber reached for the plate of food. "What are you not saying?"

"The royal guard is rounding up not only the Baron and his family—extended or otherwise," Luke answered. "They have detained and are questioning members of their clan."

"That's good news, right?" Kimber asked, diving into the chow mein on her plate.

Silence.

Slowly, Kimber started to count in her head and chewed her food.

"There is no sign of Suzette in Barrastu," her brother began.

Lifting her attention off the food, Kimber turned to Jagger as the once delicious noodles in her mouth turned to something between cardboard and sawdust.

"We think she too was on the flight with her brothers," Xavier finished.

Kimber forced the food in her mouth down and was positive it had landed like a rock in the pit of her stomach. Suddenly her appetite was lost. She placed her plate and the chopsticks on the coffee table and wasn't sure what to think.

"What's the plan?" Kimber asked in hesitation. She turned to Mikhail. "You want me to leave, don't you?"

Greif etched in Mikhail's handsome face. "Kimber, please understand."

How could she have such bad luck?

She stood and stepped away from the group, then looked back at the men. "No." She focused on Jagger. "Was this your idea or Mikhail's?"

"Kimber, these people are not be toiled with," Jagger stated tersely.

"And you forget yourself! I'm just as much as a wolf as you!" she snapped at him in a temper. Her stomach rolled as if there was suddenly a roller coaster inside. A cyclone of emotions whirled inside of her, and she was thankful the layout was identical to Mikhail's suite.

Her stomach burned and started up her throat. It was then Kimber ran to the bathroom because she would be sick.

CHAPTER NINE

Mikhail

Kimber wasn't happy, and by the way, she took off toward the bathroom. He suspected she was sick. The door slammed. Mikhail wanted to go running after her but knew she needed a moment to catch her breath. On the bright side, finding the woman he was destined to be with had been easy. However, despite him being a prince, their story turned out to be less than a fairy tale.

"You look like you've just taken a punch to the gut," Nicco told him.

Frustration and concern worked over Mikhail. "I feel like I have been," he confessed. "She is so strong and vibrant, and for a split second, when she raised her voice to Jagger, she resembled a scared girl."

"Part of its hormones," Rourke stated. "Cammie's had some mood swings."

"And the other part?" Luke asked the question on Mikhail's mind.

Rourke sighed. "She's a pregnant woman in a room with men and doesn't feel like she has an ally. Kimber has found the man she wants to spend her life with, and their lives are in danger. My guess is she is feeling a bit isolated, and a whole lot outnumbered."

"Forgive me, but she's not only the future queen of Barrastu but carrying my heir. I want her safe," Mikhail stated and darted a glance in the direction of the powder room. "And she barely touched her food."

"Hailey is having twins and was sick quite a bit," Jagger informed as he stood and walked over to the bar and removed a can of ginger ale from the mini-fridge. "Did she eat or drink when you two took time to catch up?"

"Pineapple juice," Mikhail stated. "There are a lot of vitamins in it, which is good."

Luke's phone rang, and Mikhail's nerves went on edge. Most likely his father, restless, he stood and walked over to Rourke. Her cosmetic bag is in the bedroom bathroom in our suite. I know she has a toothbrush in there. Could you please grab it for her?" he asked and reached into his jeans pocket and removed the key card.

"Of course," he replied, removed the key from Mikhail's hand, and hurried to the door. Without a glance back, he exited the suite.

"Yes, your highness, I understand. I will be sure to let your son know. We have both him and the future princess secure for now," Luke stated into the phone. "She is indeed lovely." There was a pause. "Of course, hang on." Luke turned to Mikhail. "Your father wishes to speak to you."

Mikhail refrained from groaning aloud. And took the phone. "Yes, father?"

"The Saracen clan is being held, some have talked, and the Baron himself admitted Suzette is with her brothers. AS to the intent is to have you come to your senses and return home with you. The royal guard and my Chief have indicated that all five Saracen are treated as armed and dangerous. Las Vegas law enforcement knows they are to be stopped by any means necessary."

Mikhail's anger boiled. "I told you she was hateful and cruel."

"How are things with Kimber?" his father asked, disregarding Mikhail's comment.

Considering Mikhail hadn't spoken to his father since the night before, upon arriving in Las Vegas, he was curious how he knew the gorgeous female wolf shifter's name. Luke most likely mentioned it in a prior conversation. However, he thought back to the one lingering question on his mind. "How did you get referred to Blackheart, Lombardi & Kirsch Attorneys at Law?"

There was a moment of silence, which meant his father debated his response. "I had you followed on your first trip out."

His heart stopped, and the world around him began to blur. "Who all knows?" Mikhail tried to use his brain, which currently ran on overload. "To what extent did you have me followed?" he asked, becoming more fearful by the ticking second for Kimber's safety.

"I didn't have an identification on the girl," his father admitted. "The pictures weren't much to go on."

Mikhail's body turned numb. There were pictures of Kimber.

"I went through diplomatic channels." His father's reaction and words weren't what Mikhail was expecting. "Your Aunt Ina comes from royal blood in Denmark, and her grandfather is friends with a man who is a dragon shifter. They suggested I reach out to the law firm with resources to aid shifters. Imagine my surprise when the lady you'd spent time with was a Blackheart. Very prestigious lineage. Be safe, now put Luke back on."

His blood turned to ice, and for once, he didn't care his father had gone back to giving orders. Mikhail could see the concerned expressions on the other men in the room's faces. "I blame you for this," he confessed to his father.

Before the king could respond, he held the phone out to Luke as Rourke re-entered the room.

"You're not looking very well," Rourke stated.

"Forgive me, Your Highness, but it's a little late to send back up," Luke snapped, not hiding his temper. "Go be a king, and make sure the Saracen never sees the light of day and let me ensure your son and his future wife come out of this alive." He ended the call and sighed.

Rourke passed Mikhail the key card and Kimber's cosmetic bag. "What the hell?"

Mikhail shook his head, crossed the floor, and then knocked on the powder room door. "Il mio cuore, I have your toothbrush. Please, open the door."

"Just pass it in," she told him in a weak voice that broke Mikhail's heart. The door opened a crack, enough for him to pass the bag through. The protective animal beneath his skin wanted to push open the door and never leave her side. Instead, he held back and slipped the bag through the crack. "Thank you," she stated before she again closed the door and turned the lock.

Sighing, Mikhail turned away from the door and knew the woman who he cherished and was indeed his heart was as stubborn as he was. She had to come out sometime and didn't want to incur more stress than required. He stepped away from the door then walked over to the bar.

"You look like you could use a drink," Jagger stated.

"Indeed," he answered. "Scotch, please," he replied.

The other four men joined Mikhail and Jagger at the bar. Mikhail glanced at the Chinese food and had lost all appetite. "The last time I was here. My father had me follow. He has pictures of Kimber. He never tipped his hand to the fact when I told him I was returning here."

"Damn," Nicco whispered as Jagger passed Mikhail a highball glass.

"With the security breach, there is a high chance they not only know where I stayed, but what Kimber looks like," Mikhail informed the others before taking a large sip of his drink.

"Do they know my name?" Kimber asked quietly from behind them.

Mikhail placed his cocktail on the granite surface of the bar and turned to the woman he was terrified of losing. "Most likely," he replied.

Kimber nodded, then closed the distance and threw herself against Mikhail's body. His arms went around her, and he held her close to his body.

"I promise I'll keep you safe," Mikhail assured her and placed a kiss on the top of her head.

Now he just needed to figure out how to do that.

CHAPTER TEN

Kimber

Kimber was determined to get some food into her. Not that she felt like eating, but considering the baby inside her meant everything to her, as much as the man who put it there. She wanted to give the future heir of Barrastu the best possible chance as she sat at the table while the men made calls around her. However, Kimber spent more time pushing food around on her plate with her chopsticks than eating. She was working on her second ginger ale and debated her future.

Two things were clear.

She wanted to survive this, and two, she wanted to spend her life with Mikhail.

"How are you doing?" Mikhail asked, gently pulling out a chair and sitting at the table with her.

"As good as can be expected," she replied. "I'm feeling

frustrated," she confessed. "All I can do is sit here. I still don't know how Hailey did it. Having her life threatened, and never once did she back down. She doesn't have the luxury of a beast beneath."

Mikhail was quiet a moment, and she could tell he pondered something. "There are many different kinds of strength. Knowing you, your brother, and those friends you perceive as family, you being wolf beneath your beautiful human form, and the destined to be my mate are an animal. Hailey, from what I can tell, loves completely. Love can be one of the most powerful forces in the world."

Love? Did Kimber love Mikhail?

The answer surprised her. She did.

Phones around them went off. The fact that Luke and her brothers rang simultaneously sent a chill down her spine.

The wolf beneath Mikhail's human form flickered in his Amber eyes.

"Thanks, dad. I'll have Luke text pictures to the pack, and thank you." There was a pause. "I think that's something you and mom need to ask Kimber that question, but not tonight. I'll keep you posted."

"What did dad ask?" Kimber inquired of her brother.

Jagger inhaled a deep breath. "We can't move you, and you won't be going to California," he added without room for debate. "Downstairs on the casino floor are members of our pack."

"They're already in the hotel?" Mikhail asked in a tone that revealed he already knew the answer.

"What I'm about to say is going to be absurd and crazy," Kimber choked out.

Mikhail's handsome face was etched in grief, and she met his gaze. "I love you. I think I have from the moment I saw you I was too stupid and stubborn to realize it and now...."

"Shh," Mikhail soothed and rose from his chair. He was by Kimber's side in record time. "I know, from the moment I met you, I knew you were the one. I fell in love with you, and I'm not going to let you go. Love, at first sight, is real, as is mine for you," he whispered, then leaned in and brushed his lips against her mouth.

"Okay," Luke began and walked over to where she and Mikhail were. "Rourke has texted the wolves."

"I already have confirmation the oldest brother Allan has been spotted on the casino floor," Rourke confirmed. "Las Vegas Police department has already reached out to IIP, a division of the State Department who handles diplomatic affairs."

Jagger's cell phone rang, and he glanced at the number then swiped the screen. "Hailey, is everything okay?" He paused. "What do you mean the wolves on the mountain are acting weird?" A concerned expression worked across his face, and worry etched in his features.

Mikhail exchanged a murderous look with Luke.

Jagger listened. "Sergio is with you now. Can you please put him on?" Her brother's voice was strained.

Not good. Not good at all. Kimber worried for her friend.

"Sergio, hello, what's going on?" Jagger asked with concern. There was a slight stretch of silence.

"What's happening?" Kimber breathed.

Jagger shook his head. "I cannot thank you enough. Mike and Mark are hawks, liaison with them, and they will guide some of my family's clan to work with you. Please, keep her safe. We will wait to hear from David down in security. Excellent, and thank you, let me talk to Hailey quick, please." Jagger swallowed hard. "Hey, beautiful, I just wanted to tell you, I love you and those twins of ours more than anything. Listen to Sergio. He will communicate with my family's clan and our allies. I'll be home soon." He ended the call.

"What's going on, man?" Xavier asked, concerned.

Jagger hesitated. "Could you please go out to the cabin?"

Xavier's expression became pensive. "What about Kimber?"

"She should be fine, Sergio, the girls' hairdresser is at the cabin, and there are two strange wolves on the mountain, stalking the cabin," Jagger explained. "Also, David, Sergio's new possible love interest, is on his way up from security. According to Sergio, he will help us here."

"Do you think they divided up?" Nicco asked in hesitation. "How do you know they are strange wolves?"

"Yes, they have split up." Jagger blanched and

inhaled. "Hailey knows they are foreign because they are dire wolves."

Xavier frowned, and his brow furrowed. "I thought dire wolves were extinct."

"The animal in true form is," Mikhail began and exchanged a strained expression with Luke. "There are shifters in my country that are decedents of the dire wolves." His olive skin turned ashen. "Suzette's family is one of those packs. The Saracens are dire wolves."

"I take it this David, is a shifter?" Xavier asked.

"Tiger," Jagger replied. "Please, go to Hailey."

"I can do that," Xavier replied and walked over to Kimber. He placed a kiss on her cheek. "You stay safe."

She nodded and wished he was staying but knew Hailey probably needed him more so Sergio could correspond with the wolves on the mountain. "Tell Hailey I love her, oh, and let Sergio know I need an appointment."

Xavier flashed her one of his notorious killer grins. "I will." He turned to Mikhail. "Please, keep her safe."

Mikhail nodded and offered the other man a smile. "Without her, my life would never be the same. Several of my family's guards are tigers if it is any comfort. They are strong in battle and fearless."

"Mikhail is right," Luke assured. "I would trust them with my life."

Xavier turned and crossed the floor, then pulled the door open. "You must be David, go on in, and thank you."

"No problem, Sergio has spoken fondly of the girls. He is at the mountain," David replied.

"I'm on my way there now," Xavier told him and slipped out the door.

David walked in and was a tall, gorgeous guy with shoulders resembling a wall. "Hello, everyone," he greeted.

Luke crossed the floor to him. "Thank you for assisting." Luke then proceeded to make the introductions.

"This isn't a problem," David assured. "My grandmother was born in Barrastu."

Mikhail perked. "For your service, in aiding us. I would be honored to grant you dual citizenship."

"That is very kind of you, but I'm happy to help," David told them. "I have locked the elevators. They can't come up to this floor; however, they can go down." He turned to Kimber. "I've been informed you are a wolf shifter, however in your condition, if things get out of hand. I want you to lock yourself in the elevator and hit the elevator button to go down and once it moves, hit the emergency stop button. It will be the safest place for you."

"He's right," Rourke agreed. "My brother and I are multi-shifters. I usually shift into a lion, unless I'm, playing the panda game with my niece and nephew."

"I usually shift to a wolf," Nicco supplied.

"You shift into a panda to play with the kids?" Mikhail asked, lifting his brows. "I have a lot of little cousins who would worship you if you were a panda for them." He then turned to Kimber. "I'm starting to like your family a lot."

Kimber couldn't help but smile. "They are pretty

terrific," she admitted. "Hailey took some pictures. I'd love for you to see them."

"Let's survive this, and Cammie and I will come for a visit," Rourke told him with a smile.

Kimber liked that idea but remained quiet.

"Sergio said there are two dire wolves on the mountain. How many do you think are here?" David asked.

"Three," Luke answered. "Not only are they large, but they are also ferocious, and when they attack, they go for the kill." He paused, then continued. "One of the assailants has been spotted on the casino floor."

"Security went to remove him, and he vanished," David supplied before continuing. "And my security team has the photos of five, four men and a woman. Any idea which two are on the mountain?" David asked.

"No," Nicco answered. "How many officers did the LVMPD send?"

"Eight, four of which are shifters. Two wolves, another tiger—Jared, who's my older cousin, and his best friend a grizzly shifter." David explained. "Jared is running point for the police department and thought this was the safest course of action. My cousin wanted fighters. After all, we're dealing with foreign royalty."

Kimber's stomach rolled.

She removed herself from the chair and crossed the floor to Mikhail. He immediately wrapped a protective arm around her. "Things will be fine," he promised. "We have plenty of back ups."

Mikhail met David's gaze. "Is your cousin from the same grandmother?"

David nodded and smiled. "Yes, from my mother and aunt's side. Nonna is a tiger shifter, as are our mothers. We get it from no one strange. " He cleared his throat. "Jared has also arranged for medics and ambulances, shifter friendly on standby."

"Your service to the throne of Barrastu is appreciated and will not go unrecognized," Mikhail told him, then turned to Kimber.

"There it is," Kimber smiled despite the mild anxiety. "You sounded very regal just now and showed everyone in this room what a good man you are." Tears filled her eyes, and she knew her pregnancy hormones were getting the better of her. "Something I already knew."

He cupped her face gently. "I don't want to lose you."

"I don't want to lose you either," she replied before she stretched up and kissed his lips.

A slam of a door echoed from the hallway.

"Is there anyone in the other suite?" David asked quietly.

"No," Jagger replied.

"Then someone just entered the floor through the fire escape," he informed the group. "Are any of the trouble-makers tech-savvy?"

"Suzette's brother. The one a year older than her," Mikhail explained. "Why?"

A bleak expression etched on David's handsome face.

"Because the only way to enter is with a key card. They are designed to be exited but not entered."

A loud crash echoed from down the hallway. Both David and Rourke pulled their guns.

Kimber's stomach started to hurt, and her heart began to race.

The Saracens had just declared war.

CHAPTER ELEVEN

Mikhail

"Go," Mikhail told Luke.

With practiced ease, Rourke and Luke walked with stealth toward the door, guns aimed and ready to fire.

Nicco glanced at Mikhail, then at Jagger.

Mikhail turned to Kimber. "Do you love me?"

Kimber nodded her head, and she smiled weakly. "I do."

"Jagger?" Mikhail began. "Your father isn't here. Do I have your permission?"

Her brother studied the other man. "Will you always be faithful?"

"I wouldn't want it any other way," Mikhail confessed.

"What do you need my brother's permission for?" Kimber asked quietly.

Jagger darted a glance to Kimber, then looked back at Mikhail and his blue gaze, matching his sisters who met Mikhail's. "Your answer is the same one Hailey gave me when I asked her if she was sure being my wife was what she wanted."

"You are Hailey's entire world," Kimber stated.

Jagger's brows lifted. "I know," he told his sister. "Do you love Mikhail without hesitation or any doubt?"

"Yes," she breathed. "I wanted you to find him so that we could be together."

Jagger looked at Nicco, who shook his head in agreement. He then focused his attention on Mikhail and nodded once. That was all Mikhail needed, and he turned to Kimber. "I meant what I said. I want you and our baby. For always and forever."

Kimber's blue eyes scanned his face, and her long dark lashes fluttered. "I know. Mikhail, what's going on?"

Mikhail leaned in and brushed his lips against Kimber's while reaching for her hand. He deepened the kiss and lifted her hand. Easing out of the kiss, he opened his eyes. "This might hurt, for that I'm sorry. However, it will protect you."

"You are going to bind me to you with your bite," Kimber replied.

Mikhail sighed, and his heart raced. "There is no going back."

Kimber's blue eyes sparkled, and a small smile tugged her full lips. "Then what are you waiting for?"

"It's normal to hate the fact you know it will cause her pain," Nicco told him.

Mikhail lifted her wrist to his mouth and sunk his teeth into it. The metallic taste of her blood on his tongue was arousing as it was horrifying. They were official. She was his, and in return, he was Kimber's. He removed her wrist from his mouth and released her hand.

She lifted her wrist and looked at the bruise already forming. "How will this protect me?"

"You're marked. Other wolves will know to back off," Jagger explained.

"Other shifters will know you're mated," David supplied.

Her wrist bled a bit, and she lowered the sleeve of her sweater. Kimber then closed the distance and placed her head against Mikhail's chest. He wrapped his arms around her and held her close. Kimber never said a word, and Mikhail knew she was simply listening to his heartbeat. "Promise me," he began. "Promise me. You will heed David's advice. I don't want you shifting and entering a fight unless you have to."

Kimber lifted her head and met his gaze. "I'm a wolf too," she reminded him firmly.

"One whose, pregnant," Jagger reminded. "Marriage is about compromise. Kimber, no one is saying you can't handle yourself, but please think of that niece or nephew you carrying."

"Kimber, please," Nicco pleaded. "I almost lost Jenny. Jagger and I entered the house while a drugged-out gunman had every intention of killing her and Melanie too." Emotion edged into his voice. "It's the scariest feeling anyone who loves has to experience."

Mikhail understood more why the men were so dedicated. "Mel is Xavier's mate?"

"Yes," Nicco answered. "Kimber, promise us, please."

"I promise," she whispered. "I promise you all. I'll head to the elevator and do what David said."

Bullets fired from down the hall, and a wild cat hiss and snarl resonated.

"Go into the room. Stay safe," Mikhail told Kimber, then placed a kiss on her lips. "Never forget how much I love you."

"I love you too," she whispered and stepped back.

Around him in the melding of flesh and fur and shaking bodies. Nicco and Jagger shifted. Mikhail met Kimber's gaze and kept eye contact as he shifted into a giant wolf.

Mikhail, too was a dire wolf.

He glanced at David, who remained in human form. Kimber stepped forward and caressed his fur. Mikhail loved the feel of her gentle touch on his coat. "Come back to me safe," she whispered.

He turned and glanced at the other two wolves as growls and snarls echoed down the hall. David drew his gun, walked to the door, and quietly opened it out and Mikhail, with Jagger and Nicco, ran from the room and down the hall where his hotel suite door was wide open because the door had been blown off hinges.

"Jared, I need back up here," David spoke into a walkie-talkie. Then within seconds, a tiger roared, and heavy paws followed as they went barreling into the room war raged. Two giant dire wolves fought with a lion with amethyst eyes, undoubtedly Rourke, and a large wolf, resembling a timber wolf. By scent alone, he knew the wolf to be Luke. One of the large Saracens turned and bolted directly toward Mikhail as they entered the room.

Mikhail growled and curled his lip back as he and the others attacked. The tiger went barreling over to where Rourke and Luke fought with one of the wolves. There was no way this was going to go beyond tonight.

Mikhail wanted Kimber safe, and there was only one way to ensure that.

The Saracens would be checking out of the hotel in body bags.

CHAPTER TWELVE

Kimber

The ferocious growls and animals' barks in a bloody, ruthless battle reverberated down the hall from the suite Kimber had briefly shared with Mikhail. Her eyes closed as she leaned against the wall. The men had told her to stay there, and they'd told her to be safe.

Easier said than done. Her family and the love of her life were facing life and death. At the same time, she was alone in a room. Of course, they had attacked the room Mikhail had booked.

However, she had promised them. She would obey their request. Doing so, though, was taking a part of her soul and breaking her heart. She knew they were worried about her and the baby, especially with her being so early into her pregnancy.

Still, it didn't make standing around doing anything any easier.

The click and hum of the key card activating the lock of the suite door reached her ears. She wasn't sure if it was one of the guys, who had shifted back into human form, or if one of the police officers had made it in to protect her.

The door opening then closing echoed through the hotel room. Kimber went to see who it was then her nose picked up the scent of perfume. Her feet froze and came to a halt.

"Come out, come out from wherever you are," a female voice taunted.

Suzette!

"I want to meet the American slut who thought she could steal my prince charming," Suzette stated with icy disdain.

Slut? The bitch had no idea who she was talking to.

Anger kicked Kimber to turn the corner. She stared at the woman by the threshold of the hotel suite. Suzette was pretty. However, she is not any more beautiful than Kimber or her friends. "And you hauled your ass a long way from home to pick a fight," Kimber replied.

Suzette startled. "Oh, you have no idea, not this is going to be much of a fight. You can't compete with me on any level."

Kimber snorted. "I don't need to compete with you, considering Mikhail left your ass in Barrastu and came to me. Tell me, just how desperate are you? You don't handle rejection well."

"Did you think you were anything more to my future husband than a sex toy?" She stepped closer to where Kimber stood.

"You want to believe that," Kimber laughed. Be my guest. However, if you genuinely believed Mikhail was destined to be yours, you wouldn't be such a jealous bitch."

"We were promised to each other when we were children," Suzette explained, then laughed cynically.

Kimber pulled back her sleeve. Baring the mark Mikhail's teeth had left. "Then why did he bite me?"

Surprise washed over Suzette's face before pure rage sparked in her eyes. "Liar!" she screamed at the top of her lungs.

"No, I'm not," she replied. Uneasiness rocked the acid in her stomach. "Mikhail marked me. I'm his," Kimber replied in the calmest voice she could muster. "If you hadn't doused yourself in so much perfume, you'd be able to smell him on me. Mikhail may have been promised to you, but, bitch, I'm his mate."

Suzette screamed at a high pitch which then shifted to a fierce growl. "Then that is all the more reason to tear out your throat. You won't be anything when you're dead." Her body shook in a blur of flesh melding with fur. She shifted into a large light brown dire wolf. Her lip curled back, and she growled.

Kimber hated the fact she would break her promise to Mikhail and the guys. She was about to shift when the hotel room door broke down and a large bear barreled in focused on Suzette.

The wolf growled, focused her attention on the bear, and then backed up. The large grizzly popped its jaw and huffed before releasing a loud growl. He lunged toward the wolf, and the wolf snarled, Suzette attacked, and Kimber knew her window was closing fast.

She bolted toward the door and exited the room while the two animals battled it out. Kimber pressed the elevator button and noticed the other suite door had been destroyed. The growl of Suzette and a loud wolf howl resonated through the entire floor. The elevator doors opened, and Kimber hurried inside and pounded on the close door button. Heavy wolf paws hitting the ground at a run thudded against the carpeted floor.

The doors closed as Suzette lunged.

Kimber pressed the down button with a shaking hand. Tears blurred her vision, and her stomach hurt as the elevator lowered. So did the tears that had welled up in her eyes. She counted to ten and then hit the emergency stop button. The alarm sounded, and she stumbled back against the wall. Never in her life had she felt as much like a coward as she did right then.

Not even when she had left Mikhail in the hotel room eight weeks ago.

She slid down, sat on the floor, and brought her knees

up to her chest. Despite having just acted like a weakling. One thing comforted her.

Kimber had done as she was told and, in turn, kept her promise to Mikhail and the guys.

CHAPTER THIRTEEN

Mikhail

The loud cracking of wood breaking and the thud of the suite's door at the opposite end, hitting the floor, echoed down the hall. Fear immobilized Mikhail, and he sunk his teeth deeper into the hind leg of one of the Saracens dire wolves.

Jagger bit and clawed at the other Saracens brother. A violent growl from the other end of the hall ricocheted through the hallway walls, followed by bodies crashing and thudding.

Mikhail wanted to run to Kimber but heard the sounds of a bear. The dire wolf in his grasp snapped at Mikhail, and terror over Kimber's safety fueled his rage. He locked his teeth down hard and tugged. The wolf's leg snapped, and the beast howled in agony.

The fighting across the room stopped, and the tiger

stalked over and roared, then wiped at the struggling wolf, down the hall, screams, and furniture breaking haunted Mikhail. Jagger and Luke's wolf forms ran from the room to the other suite. The only way they would have left the other Saracens wolf was if he was dead.

One down. One to go.

The tiger swiped at the wolf, who continued to snarl and claw. A loud wolf howl echoed and chilled his bones. It was the sound of one dying.

A large paw with claws extended raked across the wolf's throat. The fur and flesh tore, and blood splattered.

The battle and commotion at the other end of the hall came to a stop. It was quiet. Too quiet. The Saracens wolf ceased struggling as life left him.

His animal comrades paused, and Mikhail met Luke's gaze. A silent understanding passed between them. Rourke sauntered over as a lion from the area he'd been with Jagger and Nicco. The sound of elevator doors opening snapped Mikhail back from his moment of remorse and thought of Kimber. He turned to see para-medics rushing toward the other room.

"We're going to need a stretcher, one of them called, and a body bag," A male voice he didn't recognize called.

Sheer terror ran down Mikhail's back, spun, and then bolted toward the other room.

Fear continued to fill Mikhail's heart and soul as he entered the hotel suite the group had used for the base. Furniture was broken, and blood had sprayed against the walls and furnishings

In truth, it looked like a war zone.

There lying motionless was a light brown dire wolf. By scent alone, he knew it was Suzette. Her perfume clung to the air. His body shook as he shifted into human form again. He used the sleeve of his shirt to wipe the blood from his face and glanced around.

There was no sign of Kimber.

"Where is she?" He demanded and turned to Luke while A paramedic patched up Jagger.

"She's not here," Luke replied as another medic approached him with a medical bag in hand.

Mikhail glanced to where Suzette was still motionless on the floor.

"The wolf is gone," an officer stated as the coroner unit walked in. "Looks like a bear attacked her from the markings. She bled out."

Suzette's death meant he was finally free. He knew Baron Saracens would never retaliate, as it was he and his family and clan faced the chance of the death penalty if found guilty of involvement in the threat to the royal family.

Mikhail remembered David mentioning a bear as one of the officers for backup. He turned to the officer and nodded. "If perchance, you locate the bear, please tell him the royal family of Barrastu is most indebted."

The officer nodded in understanding. "You're speaking to him," he whispered.

Emotion and gratitude worked over Mikhail. "Thank

you, now can you please help me locate Kimber Blackheart?"

"Give me just a minute." The officer told him, then stepped away and spoke into his walkie-talkie attached to his shoulder.

Rourke walked into the room in human form and stopped near Mikhail. He turned to Jagger. "I just hung up with Xavier. He's dealing with the police on the mountain. Neither of the Saracens brothers made it. Sergio is bringing Hailey into town."

Jagger blinked at him. "Please tell me. She's okay."

Rourke smiled and nodded. "She's fine. She wants her husband and for the contractions to stop."

Dread etched in Jagger's face. "She's not far enough along to go into labor," he stated with panic. "The twins aren't big enough." Panic coated his words.

"Whoa, big guy," The paramedic warned and placed a reassuring hand on Jagger's shoulder. "Breathe. Twins often deliver around the thirty-six-week mark. However, the contractions don't necessarily mean labor."

Mikhail glanced at Jagger. He could understand why his future brother-in-law was scared. "If she is, I promise they will have the best medical care known to man."

"As soon as I am done patching up your arm, you can call her," the paramedic assured him.

The officer who had revealed himself to be the bear shifter entered the room. "Your highness, come with me." He led him to the stairwell and down four flights of stairs. Then after a keycard was swiped, they entered the hotel hallway. The officer hurried to the elevator doors, where a fireman was wedging a crowbar between the metal.

Kimber had listened. He was relieved as he was surprised, already determining the Blackheart beauty was ass stubborn as himself. Mikhail also knew there was no guarantee with the bloodshed. Kimber was unharmed. Terror worked through him, and he thought of Jagger. He understood what the other man was experiencing.

The officer helped the fireman pull open the doors. A wide-eyed Kimber looked up at the three men, and Mikhail rushed forward while the officer pressed his walkie-talkie. "I need a medic," he began, but the rest of the words failed to reach Mikhail's ears. The elevator had barely passed the floor, so the jump was minor as he entered the elevator to the woman he loved.

Mikhail knelt to Kimber seated on the elevator floor. She flung her arms around his neck and hugged him tightly. "Tell me it's over," she exclaimed in a watery voice as he wrapped his arms around her.

"Yes, il mio cuore," he whispered and buried his face in her hair. "They're gone. They're all gone and will never be able to hurt us."

A tiny sob filled the enclosed space. "Are you hurt? "No," he informed her. "Only, an ache in my heart, worried about you and our baby's safety," he confessed.

"We're fine. I was so scared. She was going to kill me," Kimber cried.

"You're safe," Mikhail assured. Despite how many times he'd kissed her lips, made love to her, or held her in his embrace, holding her in his arms now at this moment was the most remarkable sensation he'd experienced. "I love you," he breathed.

Kimber's embrace tightened. "And I love you. Can we live happily ever after now?"

Mikhail's heart warmed, and he wanted to laugh and probably would have if they hadn't just gone through a bloody and ferocious fight for their lives. "Of course, after all, you are marrying a prince."

And Kimber was not only his princess but his forever love and wolf mate.

Thank you for reading **Royal Wolf's Bride.** I hope you enjoyed the fifth book in the **Lawyer Shifter Daddies Mates** series. Mikhail and Kimber prove that love exists at first sight, and despite all odds, love that is truly destined will find a way, no matter how bleak the odds are.

Enjoy all five books in the **Lawyer Shifter Daddies Mates** series by clicking HERE.

Happy reading.

ALSO BY AMELIA WILSON

www.ingramcontent.com/pod-product-compliance
Lightning Source LLC
Chambersburg PA
CBHW071932120726
48001CB00005B/1949